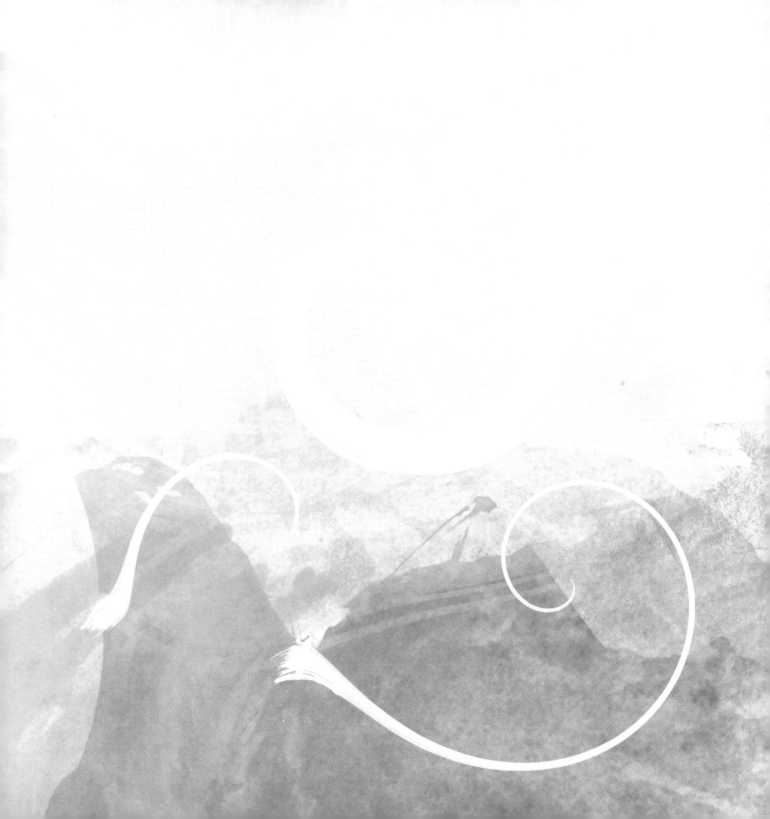

Winter is Here!

A Cake in the Morn Book

Heidi Pross Gray

For my ol'man,
who never has and never will
give up on me. Not ever,
ever, ever, ever, ever, ever,
ever!

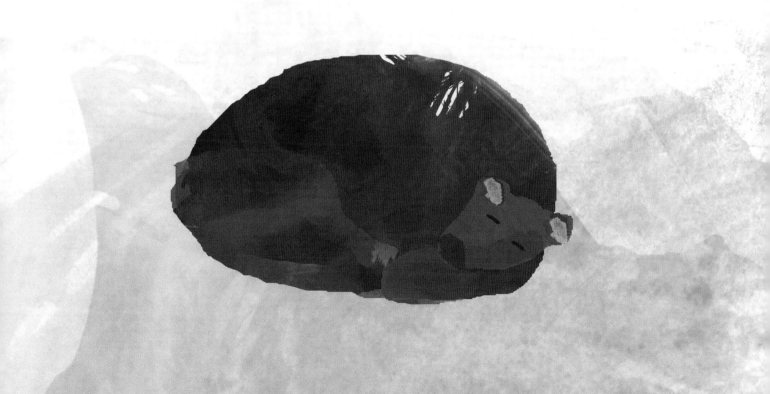

When the last leaf falls and the bare branches clatter as they play in the breeze...

Winter is here!

When sleepy animals curl together to slumber and dream until the air grows warm...

Winter is here!

When the whispering wind shares her secret that Frost is on his way...

Winter is here!

When puffs of white dance through the air, swirling and twirling at their grand snowflake ball...

Winter is here!

When evergreens stand strong, a reminder that spring will come again...

Winter is here!

When the world brings together unlikely friends to share in the bounty of the season...

Winter is here!

When you hold on tightly, zipping and sliding down the slippery, soft blanket of snow...

Winter is here!

When three balls of snow, a carrot, and some lumps of coal become your new best friend...

Winter is here!

When the untouched snow transforms into a field of brightly gleaming angels...

Winter is here!

When the sun gets sleepy before supper, leaving the night air quiet and still...

Winter is here!

When hot chocolate is the only cure for damp toes and a little red nose...

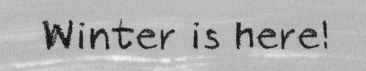

Winter is here!

When the toasty oven pops open and out marches an army of delicious treats...

Winter is here!

and when our day is over we find warmth and happiness together in our home. Winter is here!

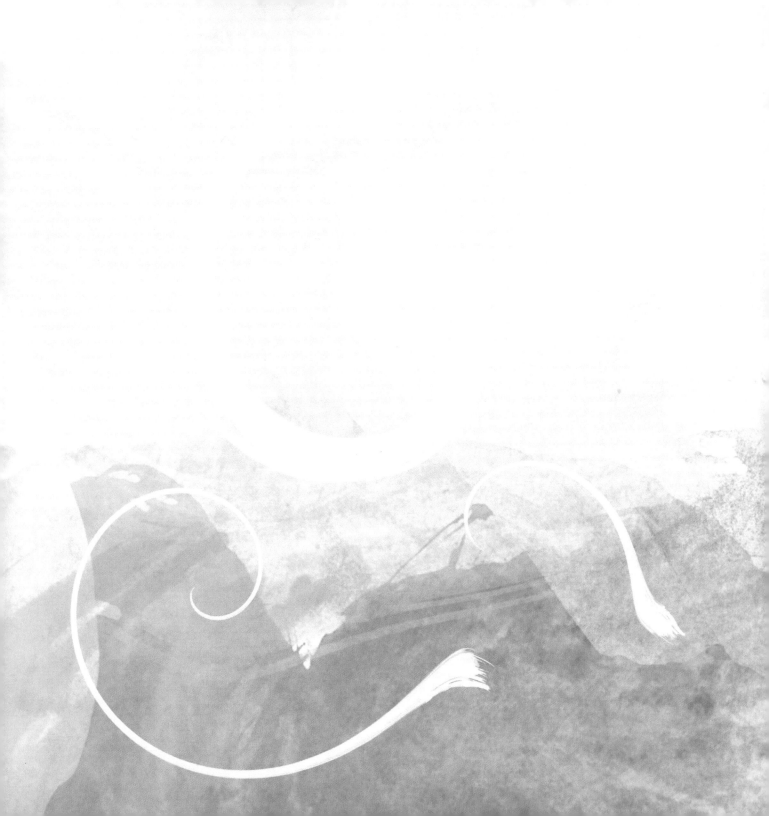

About the Author

Heidi has four kids and a husband who loves to play in the snow and then warm up with homemade hot chocolate. Heidi loves the sound of the snow falling and the fire crackling in the fireplace. After a snowfall, Heidi is the first one outside to hear her footprints crunch in the snow!

Collect all of Heidi's books about the seasons!

Autumn is Here
Winter is Here
Spring is Here

Discover Heidi's newest book, *Grandpa and Me*, which takes you on a nature walk through the woods. What will you discover?

To learn more about Heidi, purchase books, and to visit her Montessori toy store, come to Cake in the Morn at www.cakeinthemorn.com.

Made in the USA
Lexington, KY
03 December 2014